Scarlet SILVER

The Impossible Island

Original concept by Sarah McConnell
Written by Lucy Courtenay
Illustrations by Sarah McConnell

Hodder
Children's
Books

A division of Hachette Children's Books

Pleas

tel

Nor

NW
8)212

Collect all six exciting adventures:

1: Swashbuckle School

2: The Impossible Island

3: The Matey M'Lad

4: Freda the Fearless

5: The Loony Doubloon

6: The Vague Vagabond

Contents

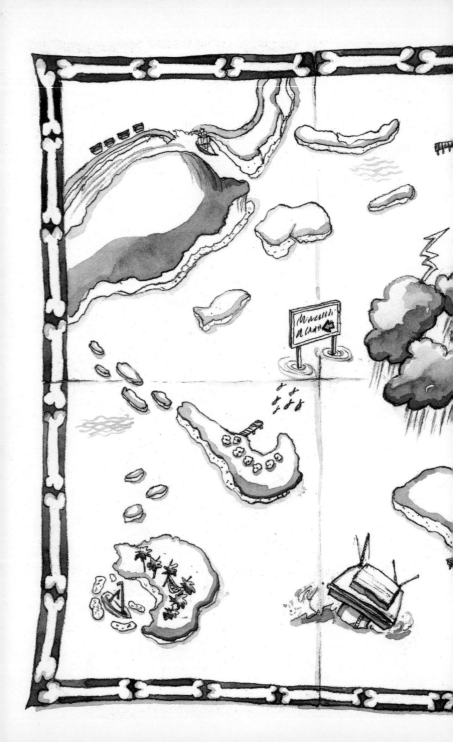

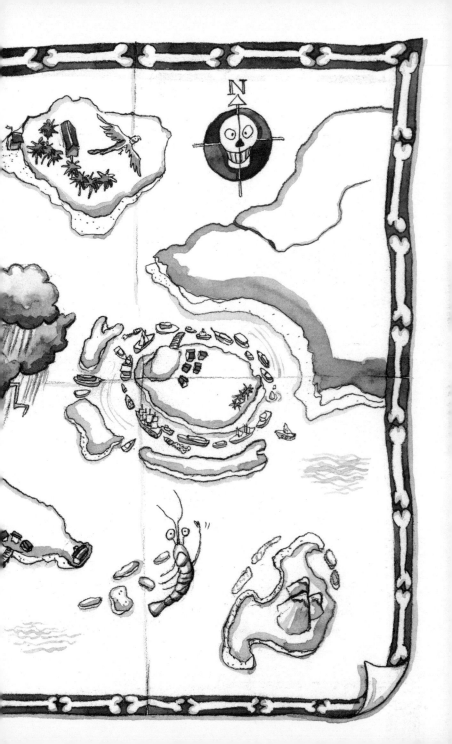

Plain Sailing

The sun blazed down on the deck of *55 Ocean Drive*. The portholes glinted like diamonds. The washing that hung in the ship's rigging was dry and stiff. All around the ship, the sea shone like a smooth blue mirror and there wasn't a sniff of wind.

It was perfect weather – apart from the wind bit. Because when you are sailing a pirate ship, wind is pretty important.

There had been no wind for five days

now. The sails of *55 Ocean Drive* hung like wet flannels in the masts. The air felt thick and hot. Even Dazzling Doris, the ship's wooden figurehead, looked a bit limp.

Up in the crow's nest, Scarlet Silver took off her black pirate hat and mopped her forehead.

"This isn't good, Bluebeard," Scarlet said to the small blue budgie perched on her hat.

"Aye aye, captain," squawked Bluebeard.

"We're supposed to be a *pirate* ship," Scarlet said. She pulled a pair of skull-shaped sunglasses out of her pale blue pirate coat and put them on. "How can we do piratey things like search for Granny's tremendous treasure if we aren't even *moving*?"

Bluebeard scratched his head with a ruffled wing.

"Exactly," Scarlet sighed.

She looked down at her crew on the deck below.

Her dad Melvin was making paper aeroplanes from the business pages of the *Pirate Post*. Lila, Scarlet's mum, was polishing the piano keys on her accordion. Grandpa Jack and his best friend One-Eyed Scott were fishing (as usual). The ship's parrot, Lipstick, was

asleep on the yardarm with his head
under one bright red wing. And lying flat
on the deck, Scarlet's little brother Cedric
was having a staring competition with
Ralph, the ship's cat.

Scarlet frowned. Part of Ralph's tail was
smoking gently.

"Festering frogs!" Scarlet gasped,

12

grabbing
a rope.
"Cedric!
Take off your
glasses, pronto!"
"But I'm
winning,"
said Cedric,
not looking
up from his
staring match.

"Ralph's going to blink any minute now."

"Cats never blink, Cedric," Scarlet
shouted, spinning down the rope towards
the deck. "Everyone knows that. Take
them off NOW!"

"Why?" Cedric asked crossly.

Scarlet landed on her feet and
launched into a flick-flack down the deck.

13

"Because the sun …" *flick* – "is setting fire …" *flack* – "to Ralph's tail …" *flick* – "through your lenses!" Scarlet finished, snatching Cedric's glasses off his nose and stamping on Ralph's smoking tail with one pointy blue pirate boot.

"MiaOW!" Ralph yowled.

"Farting fruitbats," said Lipstick, waking up and ruffling his feathers in a grumpy manner.

"What's the matter with Ralph?" Lila asked. "He ran up that mast like his tail was on fire."

Scarlet folded her arms. "I want to call a meeting of the crew," she said.

Cedric put his glasses back on and strapped on the leg splints that he wore to help him walk. Reluctantly, Grandpa Jack and One-Eyed Scott put down their fishing rods. Lila laid her accordion to one side. Melvin made one more paper aeroplane and then put his newspaper away.

Everyone stood in front of Scarlet.

"Lipstick!" said Scarlet, pacing the deck with her hands behind her back. "Come and tell us the riddle Granny taught you about the tremendous treasure, again."

Lipstick fluttered down from his perch and landed on Lila's shoulder. Lila gave him a banana.

"Underwater, overboard," said Lipstick, between mouthfuls of banana. "Up on high and wave the sword. Solve the riddle at your leisure, come and find tremendous treasure. Rar!"

"We don't understand a word of it," said Lila with a shrug.

"It's impossible," Cedric said.

"Wake up, you lazy lugabouts!" Scarlet said, stamping her foot. "Where's the Silver spirit? The famous Long Joan Silver didn't teach her parrot Lipstick a riddle about tremendous treasure so we could all sit around and make paper aeroplanes."

Melvin blushed.

"The fabulous Long Joan Silver didn't get eaten by a giant shrimp on her last pirate voyage so that we could loll about on her old ship and top up our tans!" Scarlet continued. "She taught Lipstick that riddle so we would work it out and search for her tremendous treasure! Are you with me?"

"Yes!" said Cedric.

"Ar!" said One-Eyed Scott.

"Aye, captain!" shouted everyone else.

"So," Scarlet said. "Any ideas?"

"Perhaps it means the treasure is at the bottom of the sea," said Cedric.

"Maybe it's a fish," Grandpa Jack said, brightening. After his family, fish were Grandpa Jack's favourite thing.

Scarlet spread her arms. "There's

hundreds of miles of water in the Seven Seas, and thousands of fish," she said crossly. "How are we going to find the tremendous treasure based on that?"

Everyone looked gloomy.

Suddenly one of the sails flapped noisily overhead. Scarlet looked up. Another sail flapped. Now all of *55 Ocean Drive*'s sails were billowing with air. The Silvers and One-Eyed Scott scrambled to their feet. Wind meant that they could finally start moving!

"Which way, captain?" Lila said.

"Anywhere but here!" said Grandpa Jack happily.

"And away from that pinstriped prawn of a pirate, Gilbert Gauntlet," growled One-Eyed Scott.

"I can't believe we fell for Gauntlet's

tricks on Swashbuckle Island," said Melvin, grabbing a rope and pulling. Two more sails dropped down from the mainmast. "We gave him nearly all our money for pirate lessons, and ended up working like slaves for his poxy pirate business!"

"I don't think there's anyone left at Gilbert Gauntlet's pirate school," Cedric grinned. "Everyone got away. He'll have to find some new way of stealing money."

55 Ocean Drive began moving smoothly through the water.

"Gilbert Gauntlet IS history," said Scarlet, steering the ship's wheel. "Right now, we're the ones who rule the waves. And it's time we started this tremendous treasure hunt for real!"

Gridlock!

55 Ocean Drive sped through the clear blue waters of the Seven Seas. Scarlet stood at the prow with one crimson pirate boot resting on the railings. The crimson boots were Scarlet's second favourite pair. They had gold skull-and-crossbone stitching down the sides and shiny gold buckles. It felt wonderful to have the wind whistling past her pirate hat. Scarlet had always dreamed of being captain of a pirate ship just like her granny, and now she was doing it. They'd work out the riddle and find the tremendous treasure in no time.

After all, Scarlet told herself, *no one ever said pirating was easy.*

"Land ahoy!" Cedric shouted from the crow's nest.

Everyone rushed to the side of the ship.

"That ain't land," said One-Eyed Scott. "That's traffic."

The horizon was crammed with ships. Enormous trawlers, big galleons, middle-sized yachts, small fishing boats and tiddly dinghies stretched into the distance. Everyone was fighting to get through the jam. The sound of scraping hulls and angry voices floated across the water.

"You're bumping my prow, you prancing prune!"

"Then you shouldn't be in the way, you wimpy old washtub!"

"Galloping groats!" Scarlet gasped. "How are we going to get past?"

55 Ocean Drive sailed up slowly behind a smelly little tugboat. Stinky diesel fumes floated on to the deck, making Ralph cough. Scarlet waved her hand in

front of her nose. Now there were pongy old fish smells as a very dirty fishing boat tried to push past *55 Ocean Drive*.

"What can you see, Cedric?" Scarlet yelled up to the crow's nest.

"I'll come down and tell you!" Cedric yelled back.

Cedric had just fixed two new sliding gadgets to his leg splints. Now he hooked the sliding gadgets on to the rope which stretched from the crow's nest to the deck. Then he launched himself into the air.

"Brilliant," said Lila as Cedric whistled through the air.

"He looks like a supersonic ski-jumper," said Grandpa Jack.

Cedric landed, unhooked himself and stood up. "There's about a million ships all going around this one island," he said.

"Like a roundabout or something."

Scarlet pulled out one of Long Joan's
sailing charts and laid it on the deck. It
showed a group of islands.

"We must be here," she said, pointing

to a patch of water. "And that island must be Traffic Island."

"I can see why it's called that," Melvin said staring at the jam of ships.

A little green speedboat nipped in underneath *55 Ocean Drive*'s nose.

"Cronky old cabbage-crate!" One-Eyed Scott shouted furiously.

"All the little boats are overtaking us," Cedric complained.

Lila shook her head sadly. "There'll be an accident soon," she said.

KKRRAANNGG!!!

Scarlet felt *55 Ocean Drive* shudder. Her hair stood on end under her pirate hat.

"Hard a-port!" Scarlet shouted.

"What?" said Lila, who was standing at the ship's wheel.

"Left, Mum!" Scarlet yelled. "Turn left now! A *lot*!"

"We've got a breach in the hull to starboard!" Grandpa Jack bellowed.

"*What?*" said Lila.

"There's a HOLE in the SHIP on the RIGHT-HAND SIDE!" Melvin shouted, rushing past Lila. "Turn LEFT, Lila – that way we might just stay afloat!"

"Blistering banana skins!" Lipstick screeched from up on the yardarm.

"Port, starboard," Lila grumbled, swinging the wheel to the left three times. "I wish pirates spoke proper English."

55 Ocean Drive tilted hard to the left. Scarlet began to feel dizzy as the ship spun around in circles. The sky looked like the sea, and the sea looked like the sky.

CRUNCH!

55 Ocean Drive shuddered, stopped whirling and landed on something.

"Everyone still here?" asked Scarlet breathlessly, putting her hat back on.

Ralph crept out of the cabin and was sick on the deck.

"Where are we?" Lila panted.

"I don't know," said Scarlet. "But we're on land. That's got to be a good thing."

They gazed around the little beach where they had landed. Ships streamed past them, honking and tooting at each other. It was impossible to hear themselves think.

One-Eyed Scott scrambled over the railings. "Hole's not too bad," he said, peering at the side of *55 Ocean Drive*. "Couple of planks should sort her out. Then we'll be off again."

Everyone gave a feeble cheer and clambered off the ship.

"Let's go and find some planks," said Scarlet dusting sand off her trousers.

"A chandler would be good," Grandpa Jack said.

"A chandelier won't help," said Lila.

"Mum!" Cedric groaned, adjusting his glasses. "A chandler is a shop where you can get stuff for ships. Don't you know *anything* about being a pirate yet?"

A plume of smoke rose above a nearby hill into the sky.

"Smoke," said Melvin, pointing. "Look over there!"

"Smoke means people," said Scarlet. "Follow me, crew."

The Silvers and One-Eyed Scott clambered over rocks and tussocky grass,

heading for the smoke.
Ralph rode on Melvin's
head while Lipstick and
Bluebeard looped through
the sky above them.

Over the hill, Scarlet
saw a higgledy-piggledy
group of houses around a
tiny harbour. She broke
into a run down the hill.
The others puffed a bit,
but followed.

"Hello?" Scarlet called
as they reached the
harbour. "Anyone here?"

A nearby door creaked
open. Three faces peeped
out at Scarlet and her
crew.

"Show yourselves!" Scarlet commanded.

"Please," Lila added, frowning at Scarlet.

Lila, Melvin (plus Ralph), Cedric, One-Eyed Scott and Grandpa Jack clustered behind Scarlet as a red-haired man, a girl and a boy came out from behind the door. They looked like a family.

"I'd say welcome to Traffic Island," the man said, "if welcome was the right word."

"You never said nothing truer, Dad," said the girl behind him.

"You come to rob us?" asked the small boy, holding the girl's hand.

"Of course not," Scarlet said, shocked.

The small boy squinted at Scarlet. "Ain't you pirates?"

"Well, yes," Scarlet said, feeling proud.

31

"But we just need a couple of planks to fix a hole in our ship. We ran aground on your beach. Then we'll be off again."

"Hoo!" the man wheezed. "That's a good one. Off again, eh?" He turned to the girl. "You hear that, Dora?"

"Ha!" said Dora.

"Off again!" the man repeated. "You hear that, Sid?"

"I heard, Dad," said the boy.

"Hoo!" said the man again.

More doors opened. More people stepped out of the higgledy-piggledy houses. The man spread his arms. "You hear that, Traffic Islanders?" he roared. "Off again, just like that!"

Scarlet began to feel cross. "All we want is a couple of planks," she said.

The man's eyes narrowed. "You must

be rich then, eh?"

"Why?" Scarlet asked, suddenly worried. "Are planks really expensive?"

"It ain't the planks," said Dora. "It's the toll."

"You want to leave Traffic Island?" said the man. "Go ahead. But you got to pay a toll."

"Ar," echoed the other Traffic Islanders, who had now gathered around the Silvers and One-Eyed Scott. "Billy's right! You got to pay!"

"Who do you have to pay?" Cedric said.

"Why," Billy said, "Gilbert Gauntlet, of course! Who else?"

Making Money

"*Gilbert Gauntlet?*" Scarlet gasped.

"That mangy meerkat," One-Eyed Scott growled and spat on the ground.

"You know him?" Billy said.

"We were his prisoners for a while," Scarlet said. She lifted her chin. "Until we escaped that is."

"And he's not even a real pirate," Melvin added. "He's just a builder who once went on telly in a pirate outfit."

"It totally went to his head," Cedric said.

"Before he went to sea, he built a marina that fell down," Lila finished crossly. "And the splash *completely* ruined the mayor's hat."

"Ar," said Billy. "Sounds like Gauntlet, all right."

35

"How much do you have to pay him?" Scarlet asked.

"Too much," said Billy. He waved his hand at the peeling paint on the houses and the patched old boats in the harbour. "We don't have no money left for nothing else."

Colourful curses floated across the water towards them.

"Back up, halibut-head!"

"Back up yourself, tuna-breath!"

"But if we don't pay," said Billy, raising his voice over the traffic, "then he won't stop the ships and let us through. We have to go across to the mainland most days, see – for food and that."

"I ain't had new shoes in ages," Dora said, looking longingly at Scarlet's special crimson pirate boots.

Scarlet felt sorry for Dora. She felt sorry for all the Traffic Islanders. Her heart filled with rage. Gilbert Gauntlet was *toast*.

"Well," she said. "We're here now. We've beaten Gilbert Gauntlet once, and we can beat him again. Right, crew?"

"Right!" shouted the others.

"You gonna help us?" Sid said in amazement.

"You bet," said Scarlet. "We're going to show you how to make enough money to pay the toll and leave Traffic Island whenever you want!"

"We'll need toll money too," Cedric reminded Scarlet.

"No problem," said Scarlet. "We'll make enough for all of us!"

"Hurrah!" the Traffic Islanders cheered.

"Miaow!" said Ralph, still safely

perched on Melvin's head.

Scarlet rolled up her sleeves and put her hands on her hips. "Mum?" she said. "Dad? Get your instruments from the ship. You can busk to the passing traffic. Send people out in rowing boats to collect the money. Anyone else got an instrument?"

Some Traffic Islanders produced drums, pipes and a very battered bugle.

"We'll teach you some of our best tunes," said Lila eagerly.

Scarlet paced the harbour. "Cedric?" she said. "How's your swimming?"

"I've got two flipper gadgets I can fix to my splints," Cedric said. "I can swim faster than a dolphin when I wear them."

"Some ships have windscreens, right?" said Scarlet. "They'll be covered in seagull poo and stuff. Find some volunteers. Then swim out, climb aboard and get washing. You'll make lots of money if you do it right."

Lipstick screeched overhead.

"Take Lipstick and Bluebeard with you," Scarlet added. "They can, um – mess up any clean windscreens you see."

"What about me and One-Eyed Scott?" Grandpa Jack asked.

"Do what you're best at," said Scarlet. "Catch fish. Then we can sell it."

"Not much fish in these parts," Billy said. "They all got scared off by the traffic."

A group of fishermen gathered around Billy nodded their heads gloomily.

Grandpa Jack smiled. "I wasn't Jumping Jack Silver, holder of the You Think You're Tough Enough pirate fishing trophy—"

"For the most fish caught using nothing but a roll of string and a pair of underpants," One-Eyed Scott added.

"—for nothing, lads!" Grandpa Jack finished. "If there's fish out there, we'll find 'em. Follow me!"

Soon, the whole of Traffic Island was bustling. Melvin, Lila and their new bandmates danced up and down the quay, playing pirate classics such as *The Funky Eyepatch* and *Who's That Walking Down My Plank?* Cedric and his team took turns to swim out into the traffic and wash the windscreens and portholes, with a little help from Lipstick and Bluebeard. With Grandpa Jack and One-Eyed Scott's help, buckets of fish were soon being rowed out and sold from ship to ship. *55 Ocean Drive*'s hull had also been fixed, and the pirate ship now lay quietly in Traffic Island's harbour, waiting for the chance to leave the island.

The afternoon wore away. The sky began to soften in the evening light. Ships droned endlessly past the island, this way and that.

"Gauntlet's going to be here any moment," said Billy, checking the horizon. "If you want to leave tonight, you'd better get your money ready."

"How much have we got, crew?" Scarlet asked proudly.

Cedric dumped the money on to the quay. It made a nice pile. But after paying the Traffic Islanders for their help, the pile looked a lot smaller.

"We're going to have enough, right Scarlet?" said Cedric anxiously.

"Gauntlet charges ten golden groats every time," Billy said.

Melvin whistled. Scarlet felt faint. Ten golden groats was a lot of money. No wonder everyone on Traffic Island was so poor. It made her mad to think of giving Gilbert Gauntlet their hard-earned money. But there was nothing else for it.

Everyone held their breath as Melvin added up the money.

"Nine golden groats, six silver pennies and two brass farthings," he said at last.

Groans went up around the Traffic Islanders.

"That's too bad!"

"You're so close!"

Scarlet stared at the quay and frowned. They only needed five silver pennies and ten brass farthings. There had to be something else she could do to make the rest of the money.

Scarlet sat down and pulled off her fabulous crimson pirate boots. She looked at Dora.

"Do you want to buy these, Dora?" she said. "Only if you've still got enough money to reach the mainland tomorrow, of course."

Dora gasped. "You'd sell 'em? Honest?"

"Five silver pennies and ten brass farthings, and they're yours," Scarlet said.

"Cor!" Dora said with delight. "You're on, Scarlet!"

Scarlet ran to her family and hugged

them. They'd done it! They had exactly
ten golden groats!

"Gauntlet ahoy!" shouted one of the
Traffic Islanders.

As if by magic, the traffic on the
horizon was parting. Five speedy little
purple boats zoomed through the gap,

leading a familiar ship into the harbour of Traffic Island.

At the sight of Gilbert Gauntlet's luxury yacht with its purple sails, One-Eyed Scott muttered something so rude that a seagull lost its balance on the quay and fell into the sea.

Five henchmen jumped out of the five purple speedboats, all wearing purple T-shirts stamped with Gilbert Gauntlet's logo: a golden pirate glove clutching a wad of money. They walked over to a small ticket booth at the end of the quay. A purple and gold banner waved from the top of the booth.

The fifth henchmen was someone Scarlet recognised.

Captain Curl adjusted his pirate cap and flicked his long, shiny brown curls

over his shoulders. He climbed out of his speedboat with a heavy purple ledger in his hands.

"He's dead handsome, that fellow," Dora whispered in Scarlet's ear.

"Bald as a snooker ball under his cap, though," Scarlet whispered back.

The doors of the luxury yacht opened. Gilbert Gauntlet stepped ashore with his arms held wide. His teeth were dazzling. His shiny black three-cornered hat made his golden hair look brighter than the sun, and his pinstriped frock coat looked pressed and perfect.

"Ah," he said, looking around. "My favourite part of the day. Step this way and buy your tickets to the mainland!"

Neither Gilbert Gauntlet nor Captain Curl had seen Scarlet and her family yet.

They took their place in the queue of silent Traffic Islanders and waited.

The queue moved quickly towards the ticket booth.

"Next," said Gilbert Gauntlet, looking up from his ledger.

"If you was a fish," said One-Eyed Scott, leaning on the table and pressing his nose against Gilbert Gauntlet's, "you'd be a rotten kipper."

Captain Curl and the other henchmen jumped forward and seized One-Eyed Scott by the arms. Cedric flew at them, but they grabbed him as well.

"Get off him, you silly little … *cabin boys*!" Lila spluttered.

"You aren't fit to call yourself a pirate, Gauntlet," said Melvin.

"Well, well," Gilbert Gauntlet purred,

looking straight at Scarlet as she marched up in her pink stripy pirate socks. "What a pleasure to see you again, girlie."

"Here's your money, you bloodsucking barnacle," Scarlet said, slamming ten golden groats down on the table.

Gilbert Gauntlet ran his long fingers

over the groats. "Oh, but my dear," he said with a sneaky smile. "For you, the price just went up. *Twenty* golden groats, I think. Yes, that will do nicely."

The Great Grass Tunnel

It was a gloomy gathering on the beach that evening.

Even with a warm night, a bunch of friendly Traffic Islanders for company, a crackling campfire and the smell of roasting swordfish, Scarlet found it hard to smile. She sat and watched the ships as they droned past, their lanterns shining like stars.

"We'll make the extra ten groats

tomorrow," Lila said, patting Scarlet's arm.

"Gilbert Gauntlet will just put the price up again, Mum," Scarlet said. "And again and again and again. He'll never let us leave unless we can trick him."

"I shouldn't have called him a rotten kipper," said One-Eyed Scott.

"You should have called him something *much* worse," Cedric agreed.

Grandpa Jack served up the roasted swordfish on paper plates. Everyone ate their supper in silence, apart from Ralph, who noisily chewed his fishbones. Then, after some slices of toasted coconut for pudding, Melvin took out his mouth organ and Lila took out her accordion.

"*It's small, it's brown,*" sang Melvin.

"*It rolls around,*" Lila sang back.

"The Last of the Maltesers," they sang together in tragic voices.

The Traffic Islanders began to join in.

"It's crunch, it's munch, it's after-lunch, the Last of the Maltesers …"

The melody swooshed up and down the beach like a wave.

One-Eyed Scott mopped his eyes. "A right sad song, that," he said, before blowing his nose very loudly on a dirty handkerchief.

"What are we going to do, Scarlet?" Cedric asked, stroking Bluebeard's blue and yellow feathers.

"Hmmm?" mumbled Scarlet.

"Have you got a plan yet, Scarlet?" asked Lila hopefully.

Sometimes it was a hard job being captain. But if Scarlet had learnt anything from Long Joan, it was to keep her crew's spirits up. She straightened her shoulders.

"We're going to enjoy ourselves," she said firmly. "We'll deal with Gilbert Gauntlet tomorrow. Mum? Dad? Play *The Groovy Groat*, will you? We need to dance."

It was hard not to dance when *The Groovy Groat* got going. The atmosphere lightened at once. Soon, everyone's toes were tapping. Dora danced with Grandpa Jack. Sid danced with Ralph. Lipstick did a little stomping dance in the sand, lifting his toes and fanning his tail.

"I ain't danced like that in ages," Dora

laughed, flopping down on the sand at the end.

"Traffic Islanders was famous for their dancing once," Billy added, sitting down next to Dora. "Back in the old days."

Mention of the old days brought other Traffic Islanders clustering around the Silvers. Everyone suddenly wanted to tell their stories.

"Old Creaky Dawes – that was Dora's granddad – he could open a clam shell with his teeth ..."

"Remember Old Man Hoppit, Billy? What he could do on one leg ..."

"Tell us about the Great Grass Tunnel, Dad!" said Sid, wriggling on to Billy's lap.

"What's that?" asked Scarlet.

"A very old story," said Billy, patting Sid on the head. "Way before old Creaky's time, even. Traffic Islanders never needed to sail to the mainland in them days."

"But you're an island," said Melvin looking surprised.

Billy cocked his head. "Time was," he said, "when islanders could walk from Traffic Island to the mainland and not get their feet wet. The Great Grass Tunnel, see? It went under the sea."

"An underwater tunnel made of grass?" said Cedric, looking up from sharpening the pen-knife attachment on one of his splints. "But grass isn't waterproof!"

"That's what Creaky told us," Billy said with a shrug. "A Great Grass Tunnel."

Scarlet jumped up in excitement. "But that's fantastic!" she said. "Where is it?"

"Nobody knows," Billy said sadly. "It's lost, see?"

"But if we find the tunnel, you'll never have to pay Gilbert Gauntlet again!" Scarlet said. "We'll help you look. My granny, Long Joan Silver—"

There was a hubbub among the Traffic Islanders.

"Long Joan Silver is your *granny*?" someone shouted.

"But she's famous!" someone else gasped. "The most fearless and beautiful pirate on the Seven Seas, they say!"

"They can't say it now," Cedric replied gloomily. "She died."

"Et by a giant shrimp," One-Eyed Scott added with a sigh.

"More than six years ago," said Lila.

"She came here once," said Dora. "My granddad, Creaky Dawes, fell in love with her, you know."

"I hope your grandmother didn't mind," said Lila anxiously.

"Everyone loved my Joan," Grandpa Jack said, looking misty-eyed. "She was a sight in her long velvet boots."

"As I was saying," Scarlet said. "My granny had a big chest full of treasure-hunting stuff – spades and compasses, things like that. I keep it in my cabin. I'm sure we'll find something that will help us look for your tunnel, Billy."

Billy looked excited. "You think we can really find it?" he said.

"Of course we'll find it," Scarlet said firmly. "We're pirates. Pirates find stuff. First thing in the morning, we'll meet you back on this beach. And if we don't find your grass tunnel, I'll lick Ralph's bottom clean next time he needs a wash!"

The Hunt is On!

It took all six members of *55 Ocean Drive*'s crew to carry Long Joan's old treasure chest down to the beach at sunrise. Seven if you counted Ralph, who was riding on top of the chest.

It was a relief to reach the beach, where Billy, Dora, Sid and the other Traffic Islanders were already waiting for them. The ships bustled past, smelly and noisy as ever.

Scarlet opened the large bronze padlock that hung from the chest. She flung open the lid, sending Ralph flying. Everyone peered inside.

"Wow!" Billy gasped.

"There's so much stuff!" Dora said.

No one had ever seen so many pirate gadgets.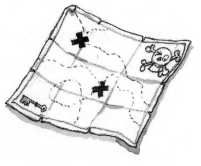

"Mum was always well organised," said Lila proudly.

"A map!" said Sid, seizing on a folded piece of paper that lay at the top.

"It's a skeleton treasure map," Scarlet explained. "You can use it on most basic treasure hunts."

"Maybe we could use it to find Mum's tremendous treasure," said Lila in a low voice to Scarlet.

"I've already tried," Scarlet whispered back. "But it can't answer riddles. Too complicated."

"Underwater, overboard," said Lipstick, at the word 'riddle'. "Up on high and wave the sword."

"Let the sounds of the Seven Seas soothe you," Billy read slowly from the back of a CD. "The clash of steel, the shout of battle, the crash of waves, the song of whales."

"Inspirational pirate music," Grandpa Jack said. "Joan loved it."

More and more things came out of the chest: a silver compass engraved with a cross-eyed mermaid; a snorkel for finding treasure on the seabed; an iron spade with a skull for a handle; a telescope on legs shaped like fish tails.

Even Scarlet had forgotten half the things inside her grandmother's chest. She pulled out a strange square pendant on a long golden chain and held it up to the light. She heard her grandmother's voice echoing in her mind.

"Take care of that, Scarlet. There's an adventure behind it."

The pendant was made of green enamel, with thin blue stripes that wiggled across it like worms. The colours had always reminded Scarlet of an island criss-crossed with streams – although she'd never seen an island with square edges.

"Underwater," Lipstick suddenly squawked from Lila's shoulder. "Underwater, rar!"

"No Lipstick," said Scarlet, putting the pendant around her neck. It matched the green pirate coat she was wearing. "We're still on the beach."

Melvin started handing out things to help them hunt for the tunnel. Dora took the mermaid compass. Sid nervously took the spade with the skull handle.

Cedric fixed a speed-digging gadget to one of his splints. He tested it and nearly disappeared as the gadget whirled a hole straight down into the sand.

"Where do we start looking?" Dora asked in excitement.

"Along the shore that faces the mainland," Scarlet suggested. "Check the grassy dunes extra carefully."

"Aye aye, captain," said Melvin.

"Just like the old days," Grandpa Jack chortled, slinging a large spade over his shoulder and striding off.

One-Eyed Scott started singing under his breath and waving his elbows in a peculiar manner.

"Save *The Funky Eyepatch* for later, One-Eyed Scott," said Scarlet, tucking her pendant safely inside her frock coat and

feeding Bluebeard a sunflower seed.

"We've got work to do!"

The Silvers, One-Eyed Scott and the Traffic Islanders fanned out. Scarlet took the section closest to the harbour, together with Billy, Ralph and several Islanders. Lila took Cedric and a group of children to where *55 Ocean Drive* had run aground. Lipstick flew overhead, screeching "Bottoms!" and making the children laugh. Melvin took Dora, Sid, some of Sid's friends and their parents to the other side of the harbour. Grandpa Jack and One-Eyed Scott decided to hunt at the furthest edge of the shoreline, where a coral reef stretched out into the sea.

The sun climbed steadily in the sky. As the day grew hotter, the smell from the passing traffic grew worse. The searchers dug and searched and searched and dug. But the grass tunnel stayed hidden.

As evening approached, Scarlet took off her pirate hat and fanned herself with it. The ships' fumes were making her dizzy.

She glanced anxiously at Ralph. His bottom was starting to look rather sandy.

Melvin appeared, followed by Dora, Sid and their straggle of searchers. "Nothing," Melvin said sadly.

"Except a spoooooooky spade," said one of the Traffic Island children, making googly eyes at Sid.

"Young Sid says the skull on his spade winked at him," Melvin explained.

"It *did*," Sid howled.

"Nothing here either," Scarlet said. "Let's go and see how Mum's getting on."

Over the hill, Lipstick was flying upside down with cackles of glee. Lila was completely buried in sand, with only her head showing. Cedric and the other children were building sandcastles.

"What," Scarlet thundered, "are you doing, Mum?"

"Um," said Lila, as Scarlet stood over

her with her arms folded. "We didn't find anything, so Cedric thought he'd show us how quickly he could dig a hole with his speed-digging gadget and, er ..."

"Don't you realise how important this is, Mum?" said Scarlet crossly. "If we don't find this tunnel, I'll have to lick Ralph's bottom clean!"

"Urgh!" Cedric screwed up his face. "Will you really?"

"I gave my word," said Scarlet. "And a pirate's word is law."

Lila struggled out of her sandhole. "Perhaps Grandpa Jack and One-Eyed Scott have found something," she said in a sheepish voice.

Scarlet marched down to the coral reef.

"Nothing here, Scarlet," said Grandpa Jack, looking up guiltily from his fishing rod and blushing.

"Honest," said One-Eyed Scott, opening his one eye as wide as he could. "We looked and everything."

Scarlet put her head in her hands.

"Don't worry," said Grandpa Jack. "I'll catch us a nice fish and—"

"I don't want fish," Scarlet shouted. "I want to beat Gilbert Gauntlet! And then I want to get off this island and look for Granny's treasure! Am I the only person here who's thinking about that?"

Scarlet turned to face Billy and the other islanders, who had joined them at the reef. "I'm really sorry, Billy," she said. "We haven't found your tunnel."

"At least we know how to make money now," said Dora. "We'll get to the mainland at least twice a week."

"Let's forget about Gilbert Gauntlet and have a bit of lunch," said Lila.

"There's a nice big catfish down off this reef," Grandpa Jack said, peering over his rod at the water. "But my hook keeps hitting something every time I try and catch it. It's like there's a sheet of glass down there or something."

Scarlet spun around. "*Glass?*" she said.

Grandpa Jack shrugged. "Just what it feels like," he said.

A fantastic idea had struck Scarlet. "Billy," she said. "Could your legend be about a *glass* tunnel, not a grass one?"

Billy frowned. "Old Creaky did have a bit of a lisp," he said.

Scarlet grabbed the pirate snorkel and scrambled on to the coral reef. She leaned over the sea as far as she dared

and gazed into the water.

"BUST MY BRASS BUCKLES!" Scarlet
shouted, lifting her head. "I *can* see glass!
It's a GLASS tunnel, and we've FOUND
it!"

Escape

There was uproar.

"A *glass* tunnel!"

"Old Creaky was right!"

The Traffic Islanders rushed to the reef. The glass winked at them under the water.

"You're Captain Scarlet, the greatest pirate on the Seven Seas!" Dora squealed.

"I don't have to lick Ralph's bottom clean," Scarlet sang, doing cartwheels up and down the beach.

"Where's the mouth of this tunnel
then?" Billy asked.

Everyone rushed to grab their spades.
Sand began to fly. Cedric put his speed-
digger on full power and ploughed up half
the beach. Melvin, Scarlet and Lila carried
boulders to Grandpa Jack and One-Eyed
Scott, who piled them out of the diggers'

way. Lipstick and Bluebeard zoomed overhead. Even Ralph helped a bit.

The sun was almost touching the horizon now. Scarlet's heart lurched. A yacht with purple sails was slowly making its way towards the island, flanked by five purple speedboats.

"Gilbert Gauntlet is on his way!" she shouted in warning.

"Let him come!" Billy shouted. "We've found it!"

A black hole gaped among the boulders beside the coral reef. Everyone cheered.

Scarlet ran to the hole. Getting down on her hands and knees, she crawled inside.

To begin with, everything was dark. But suddenly, the tunnel burst with blue light. Scarlet stood up. She stared around in wonder. Little fish darted overhead.

Seaweed waved and danced beside her. Scarlet walked on, the light growing dimmer. She could see the shadows of boats passing above her head. The mainland was perhaps a ten-minute walk away into the blue-lit gloom.

Scarlet glanced up as a shadow fell across her. She froze.

A large golden glove gleamed on the bottom of Gilbert Gauntlet's yacht as it cruised by. Scarlet was suddenly aware of her bright pink pirate hat. If Gilbert Gauntlet looked overboard, he'd spot her straight away.

Tearing off her hat, Scarlet ran back to the others as quickly as she could.

"He's getting closer," she gasped, bursting out of the tunnel.

"Anyone who wants to leave the island

tonight should go right now," Melvin advised the islanders.

"There's no time to lose!" said Lila.

Cedric pushed One-Eyed Scott towards the tunnel mouth.

"Not us," said Scarlet. "We need to *sail* away. We've still got Granny's treasure to find, remember?"

"Jumping jam jars," said One-Eyed Scott. "You're right, Scarlet."

"So we have to pay Gilbert Gauntlet the toll?" said Cedric indignantly.

Scarlet tapped her nose. "Don't worry about that, little brother," she said. "I've got a plan."

The Traffic Islanders were making plans to celebrate on the mainland. Now the tunnel was open, they could go over any time they wanted.

"You'll need disguises so you're the same colour as the sea floor," Scarlet said. "The tunnel's glass, remember? Give yourself a headstart, before Gilbert Gauntlet realises that something's wrong and catches you."

Billy touched his red hair. Then he looked at his red-haired son and daughter. "Ain't no way Gauntlet's going to think we're seaweed," he said.

"Seaweed!" Scarlet declared. "Perfect! Grab handfuls of it, everyone – and put it on your heads!"

The Silvers and One-Eyed Scott scooped up handfuls of seaweed and draped it over the islanders' heads and shoulders.

"You look like sea monsters," said Grandpa Jack.

"If Gilbert Gauntlet does see you, he'll

be scared out of his wits," said Cedric.

"Gauntlet don't have wits," said One-Eyed Scott. "Nits, maybe."

Scarlet wagged a finger at Billy. "Don't let Gilbert Gauntlet make you pay a toll for your tunnel now," she said.

"Gauntlet might control the sea round

these parts," said Billy. "But he don't control our island, and he don't control the mainland neither. How's he going to make us pay?"

"Ar!" The Traffic Islanders cheered.

"The tunnel's ours," Billy said. "Whether Gauntlet likes it or not!"

Giggling and waving, everyone began to file into the tunnel. Billy, Dora and Sid were the last to go. Billy shook hands hard with the Silvers and One-Eyed Scott. Dora burst into tears and Sid hugged Ralph.

"We won't forget you," said Billy to Scarlet. Then he turned to his family. "Let's pop in to Auntie Marge's," he said in excitement. "She always used to have cake on Thursdays."

"Not with seaweed on our heads, we won't Dad," said Dora. "Auntie Marge'll murder us if we drip on her carpet …"

Lila sniffed as Billy and his family disappeared into the tunnel.

"Just us left, then," said Melvin, in the loud voice he used when he was feeling emotional.

"Not for long," said Scarlet. She pointed out to sea.

The luxury yacht with its purple sails was getting closer to Traffic Island. Scarlet could see Gilbert Gauntlet standing at the prow, his shiny black pirate hat in his hands.

"How are we going to pay Gilbert Gauntlet, Scarlet?" asked Lila.

"Gilbert Gauntlet won't get any money from us," Scarlet promised. "Don't worry."

A gust of wind made Gilbert Gauntlet drop his hat. It landed in the sea with a splash. The pirate stared down into the water – and yelled in fury.

"He's seen them!" Lila said, clutching Scarlet's arm.

The yacht was turning around. The five speedboats turned in a swirl of spray as

well, narrowly missing a cluster of fishing boats that were trying to get past.

"He's chasing them now," Cedric said.

"He'll never get any more money from them," Grandpa Jack grinned and jigged in delight.

"Never in a month of mothballs," One-Eyed Scott agreed.

"Let's get out of here while he's not looking," Scarlet said. "I know how we can leave the island—"

"Underwater," Lipstick screeched suddenly from overhead.

"No, Lipstick," said Scarlet. "I already explained. We can't leave through the underwater tunnel because we have to fetch *55 Ocean Drive*—"

"Underwater, underwater!" Lipstick repeated urgently.

"Ow!" Cedric ducked as the bright red parrot divebombed him. "Lipstick, have you gone crazy?"

"Bottoms," said Lipstick, divebombing Melvin this time. "Underwater, underwater!"

A thought burst into Scarlet's head. She

whirled around and stared at the tunnel. "Underwater," she whispered. *"He means Granny's riddle!"*

"You mean, the glass tunnel is the underwater bit of Granny's riddle?" asked Cedric in amazement.

"Granny came to Traffic Island," said Scarlet, almost choking with excitement. "It makes sense!"

Something glinted among the stones and rubble beside the tunnel. Feeling like she was in a dream, Scarlet bent down and picked it up. Lipstick stopped divebombing Melvin and settled on Scarlet's shoulder. Sitting on Scarlet's hat, Bluebeard flapped his tiny wings jealously and screeched.

"What have you found, Scarlet?" Lila gasped. "Is it gold?"

Scarlet turned the glinting object over in her hand. It was a piece of blue enamel with two straight edges and one wavy edge. The blue was the colour of the sea. It reminded Scarlet of the strange green pendant she wore round her neck.

"For skull's sake, what is it?" Grandpa Jack demanded.

Scarlet pulled the green pendant out from underneath her frock coat. The piece of blue enamel fitted neatly into one corner, straight edge to straight

edge, with a magnetic *clunk*.

"Rar," said Lipstick, and gently nipped Scarlet's ear.

Scarlet tucked the pendant inside her pirate coat and looked at her crew. Her eyes were bright.

"The riddle," she said. "It's about helping people. We helped the Traffic Islanders by finding their underwater tunnel, and then we found this. To solve the next part of the riddle, we have to find some more people who need our help!"

The Silvers and One-Eyed Scott rushed back to the harbour, where *55 Ocean Drive* lay waiting for them.

"The traffic looks worse than ever," said Melvin as they boarded the ship. "How are we going to leave the island?"

"Remember that plan I mentioned?"

said Scarlet with a grin. She ran back to the quay, where Gilbert Gauntlet's ticket booth still stood. Pulling down the purple and gold flag with its pirate glove logo, she carried it back to the ship.

"Cedric?" she said, handing over the flag. "Send this up the flagpole."

The wind filled the purple and gold flag and fluttered proudly in the breeze. Immediately, the ships that passed in front of Traffic Island stopped, leaving a completely clear stretch of water before *55 Ocean Drive*.

"Underwater, overboard," Lipstick squawked in great excitement. "Up on high and wave the sword!"

"Where to, Captain?" Lila called from the ship's wheel.

"Go with the wind," Scarlet cried. She

could almost smell the tremendous treasure. "And look out for trouble that's 'overboard'!"

55 Ocean Drive leaped forward, the wind tugging at her sails.

"*Oh a-sailing we will go,*" One-Eyed Scott sang, waving his elbows and wildly stamping his feet.

"*'Cos we're pirates head to toe,*" sang the others, stamping their feet too.

"*We don't have baths so we often smell,*
Our pants are pretty pongy
And our feet as well,
But what we do, we do darn well –
DOING THE FUNKY EYEPATCH!"

Read some of Scarlet's next adventure in
THE MATEY M'LAD

The Storm

Lightning split the air over the Seven Seas. The sky was black. The wind moaned, the rain fell and waves rose all around like unfriendly mountains.

In the middle of the storm, a strange-looking pirate ship called *55 Ocean Drive* was struggling to stay afloat. It looked like a house, but with masts and tightly furled sails. Several tiles had blown off its roof, and its window boxes were a sea of mud and wet geraniums.

A small blonde pirate in a waterproof plastic pirate hat was standing at the ship's wheel. Her beaded plaits hung down like soggy string. A square green pendant bounced on the front of her pink mackintosh. Her eyes were bright, and possibly the wettest budgie in the world was sitting on her shoulder.

"Not much longer!" Scarlet Silver shouted. She heaved the wheel to avoid a wave that looked like a cliff. "The storm will blow itself out soon. Hold on tight, Cedric!"

A very small pirate clinging to the mainmast flipped open the visor on the space helmet he was wearing. Rain spattered his glasses. "Don't worry, Scarlet," Cedric bellowed over the wind.

Swashbuckle School
SARAH McCONNELL · LUCY COURTENAY

HB 978 0 340 98912 8
PB 978 0 340 95967 1

The Matey M'Lad
SARAH McCONNELL · LUCY COURTENAY

HB 978 0 340 98914 2
PB 978 0 340 95969 5

Freda the Fearless
SARAH McCONNELL · LUCY COURTENAY

HB 978 0 340 98915 9
PB 978 0 340 95970 1

The Loony Doubloon
SARAH McCONNELL · LUCY COURTENAY

HB 978 0 340 98916 6
PB 978 0 340 95971 8

The Vague Vagabond
SARAH McCONNELL · LUCY COURTENAY

HB 978 0 340 98917 3
PB 978 0 340 95972 5

Read more of Scarlet Silver's
adventures on the High Seas